THIS WALKER BOOK
BELONGS TO:

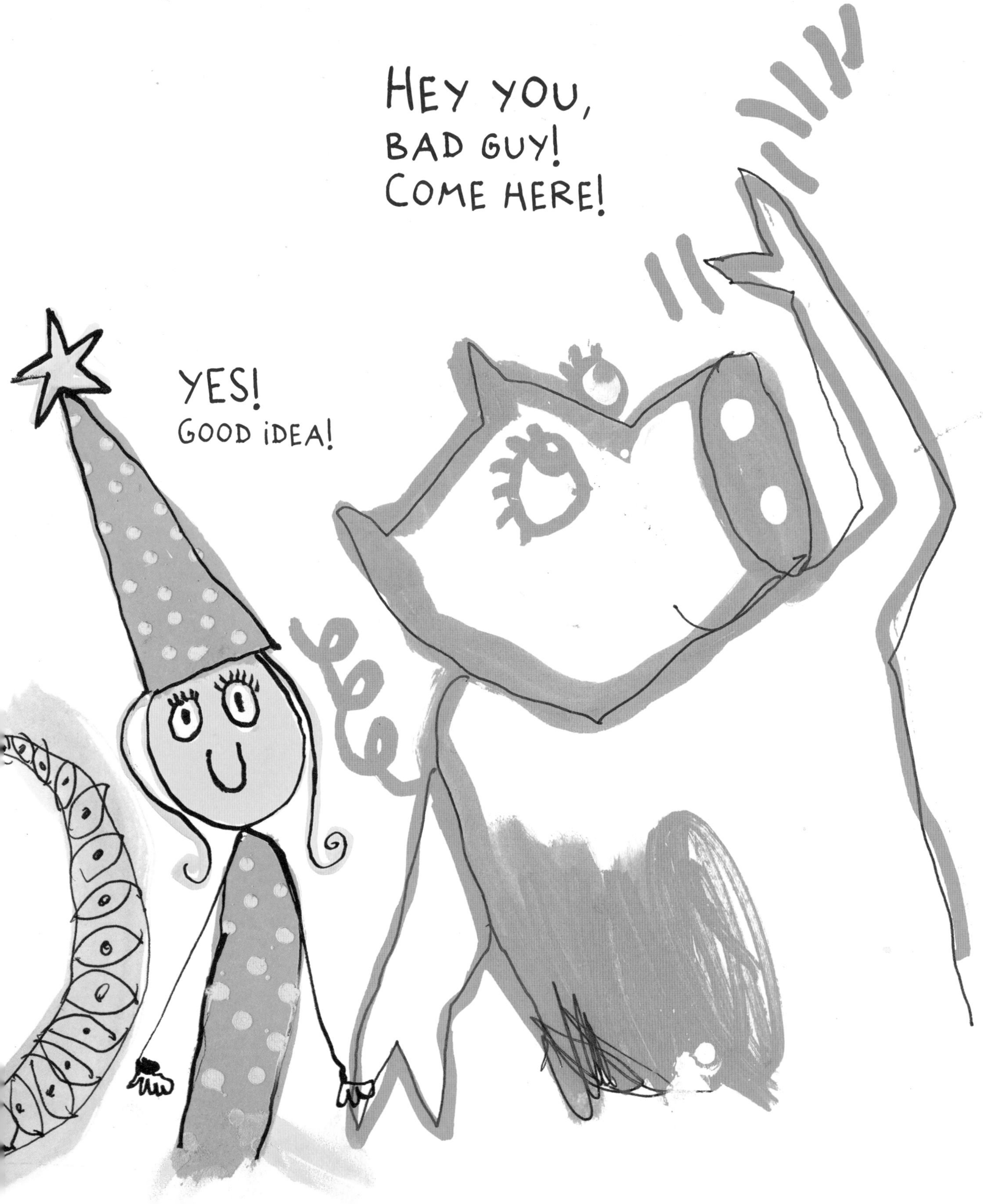
HEY YOU,
BAD GUY!
COME HERE!
YES!
GOOD iDEA!

NOW WHAT?

NAH, I DON'T KNOW ANYTHING ABOUT THAT. BUT I DO KNOW IT ISN'T VERY EASY. YOU'RE GOING TO NEED SOMEONE ELSE . . . AN AUTHOR!

HEY AUTHOR I

EVERY

AUTHO

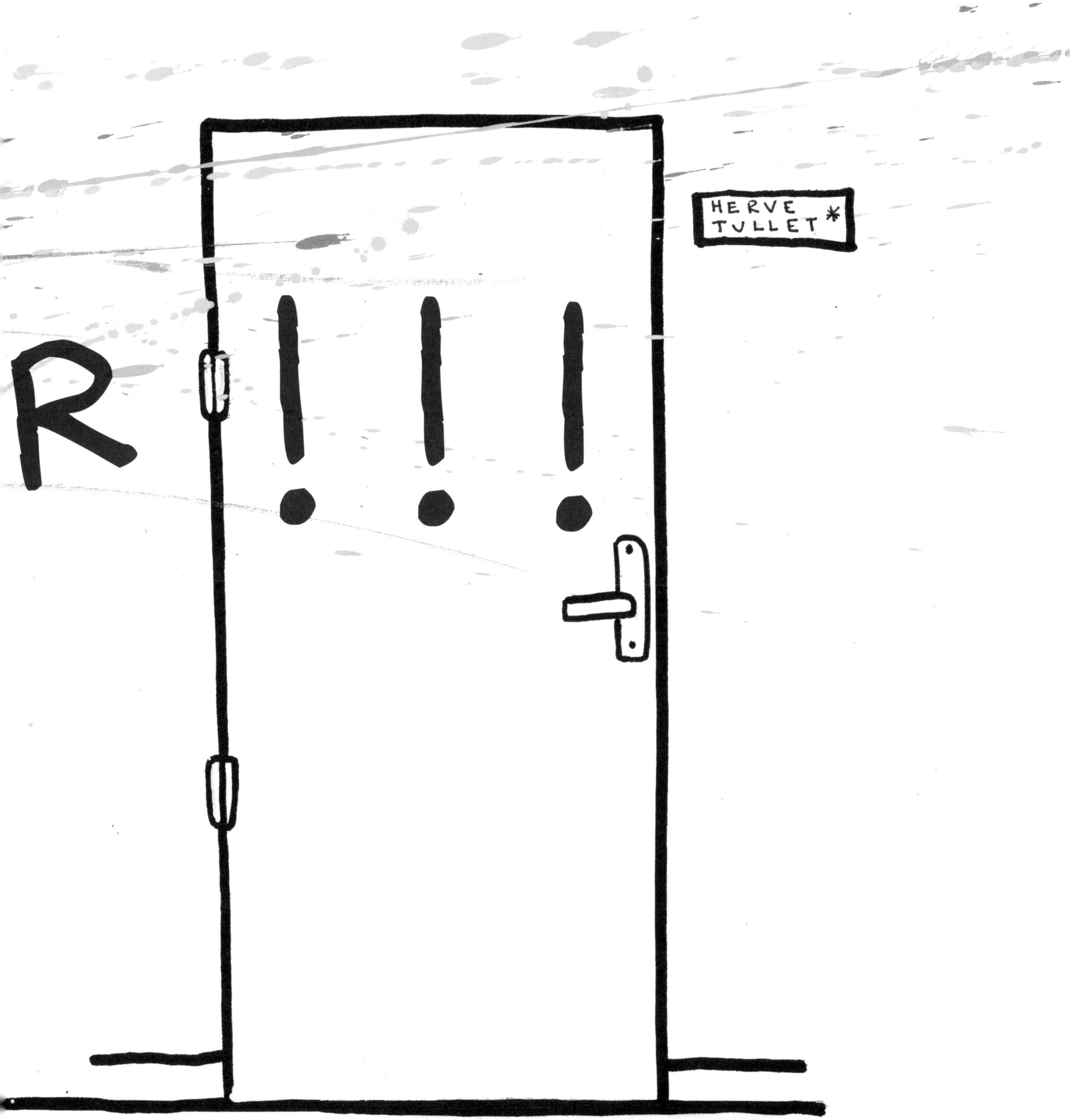
R!!!
HERVE TULLET*

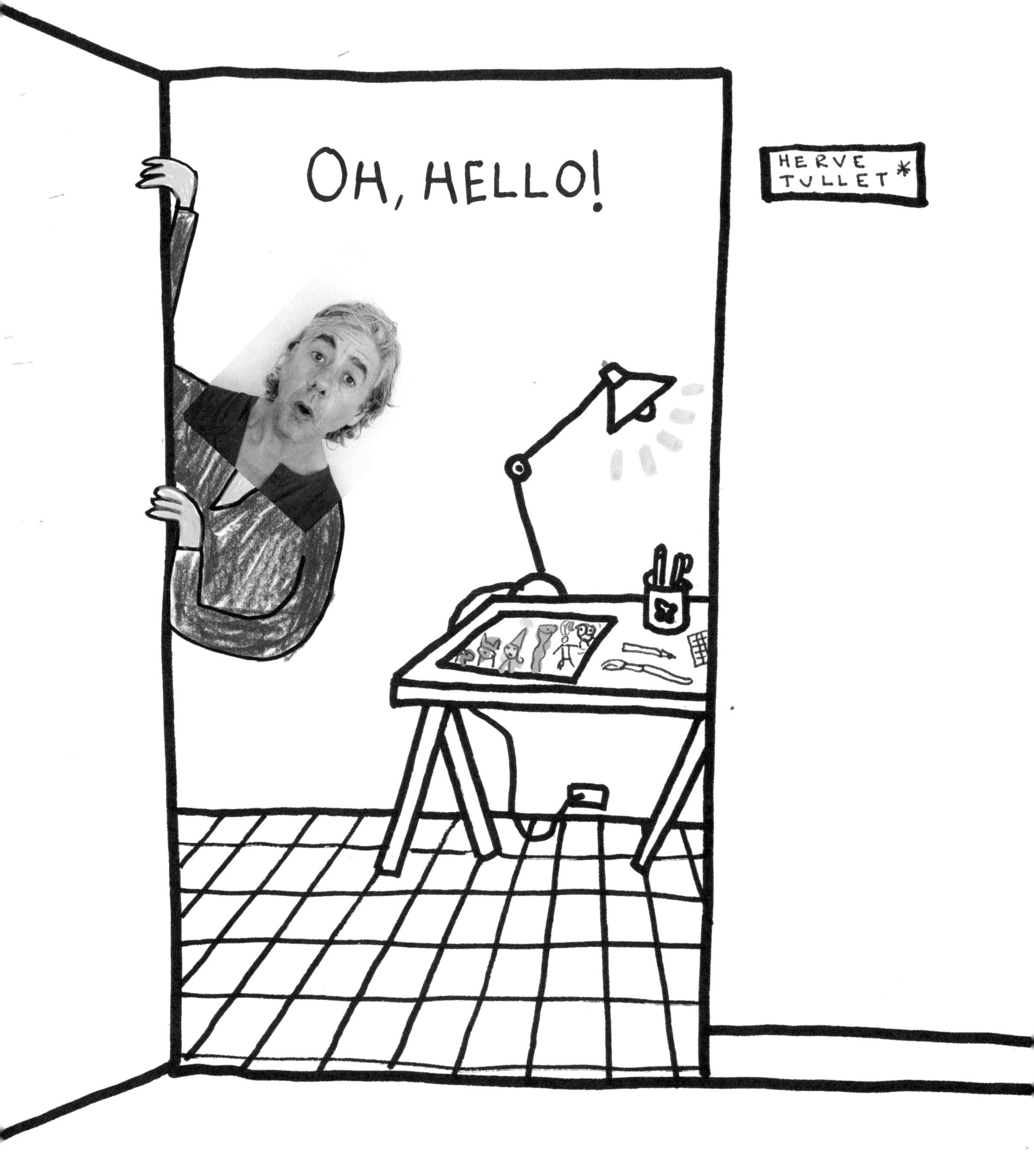
OH, HELLO!
HERVE
TULLET*

UM, HOW DID YOU GET IN HERE?

SORRY, BUT YOU CAN'T STAY HERE. I'M NOT READY. THIS BOOK ISN'T FINISHED YET!

BUT THEY **WANT** A STORY!

YOU COULD AT LEAST TRY!

THEY'VE COME SO FAR!

THEY'RE REALLY NICE, TOO. . .

AND THEY DID ACTUALLY
CHOOSE OUR BOOK!

FINE, FINE.
JUST ONE STORY. ONE TEENY, TINY STORY . . .
AND THEN YOU GUYS HAVE TO GET OUT OF HERE, OK?

Once upon a time,

on a beautiful sunny day, our heroes were walking peacefully along a road, when, all of a sudden . . .

a monster attacked them!

But the beautiful, kind fairy, who knew a magic spell and had a magic wand, said: Beat it, bad guy!

And the evil monster ~~left~~ ~~went off~~ disappeared!

WILL THAT DO?

AT LEAST
WE LOOK GOOD
IN THE PICTURES.

HMPH.

IT WAS
A LITTLE
SHORT,
ACTUALLY.

YOU COULD
HAVE TRIED
A BIT HARDER.

BUT THE ENDING
WAS . . . SO-SO.

IT WAS SO-SO?
LOOK, iF YOU'RE NOT HAPPY YOU CAN GO
AND LOOK FOR A STORY SOMEWHERE ELSE.
THERE ARE LOTS OF
OTHER BOOKS, YOU KNOW!!!

AND BEFORE YOU LEAVE, COULD YOU DO ME A LITTLE FAVOUR, DEAR READER . . .

PRESS HERE, PLEASE.

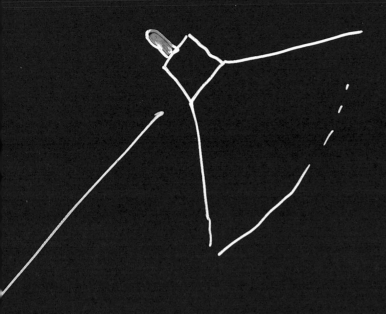

THANK YOU!
AND IF YOU SEE ANY OTHER PEOPLE,
OTHER READERS, TELL THEM
NOT TO CHOOSE THIS BOOK!

NOT RIGHT NOW, AT LEAST.
NOT UNTIL WE HAVE A TITLE ANYWAY.

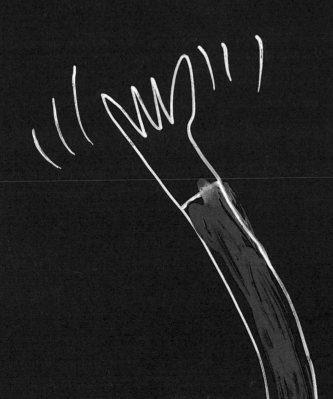

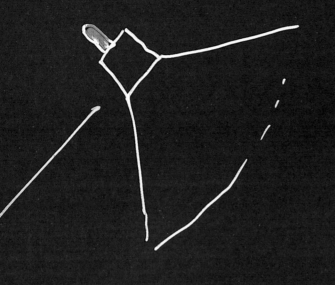

HEY, READERS,
PLEASE CAN YOU
TURN THE LIGHT
BACK ON?

OK, WE'LL SWITCH
IT ON AGAIN.
IT'S JUST HERE.

WELL, HE STILL
DOESN'T SEEM
TOO HAPPY.

 Is HE GONE?

THE END

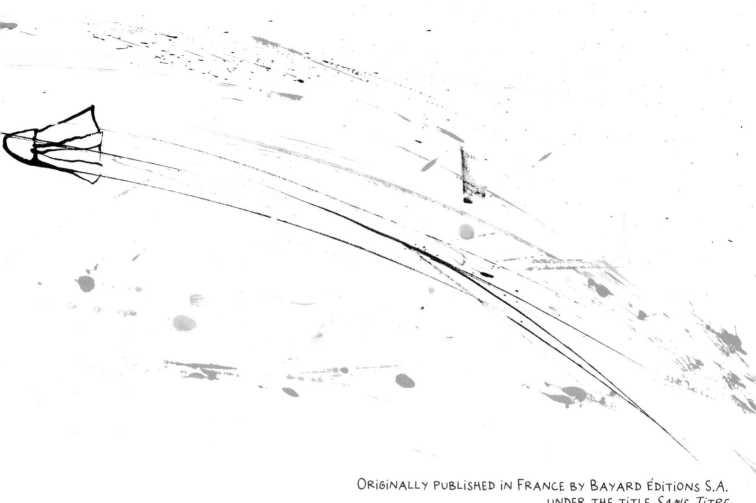

Originally published in France by Bayard Éditions S.A.
under the title *Sans Titre*

Sans Titre © Éditions Bayard 2013

First UK edition published 2013 by Walker Books Ltd
87 Vauxhall Walk, London SE11 5HJ

This edition published 2014

10 9 8 7 6 5 4 3 2 1

A big thank you to Theirry Mariat for the photographs.

The right of Hervé Tullet to be identified as author/illustrator
of this work has been asserted by him in accordance with the
Copyright, Designs and Patents Act 1988.

Translation © 2013 Walker Books Ltd

Printed in China

British Library Cataloguing in Publication Data:
A catalogue record for this book is available from the British Library.

ISBN 978-1-4063-5164-4

Visit   WWW.WALKER.CO.UK

AND   WWW.HERVÉ-TULLET.COM

HERVÉ TULLET
MAY NOT HAVE FINISHED THIS BOOK,
BUT HE HAS FINISHED LOTS MORE, INCLUDING,

PRESS HERE,
WHICH HAS BEEN TRANSLATED INTO
27 DIFFERENT LANGUAGES.
HE'S EVEN MADE IT INTO AN APP!

HERVÉ LIVES IN PARIS AND IS CELEBRATED
THE WORLD OVER FOR HIS PLAYFUL,
ENDLESSLY INVENTIVE AND
INTERACTIVE STORYTELLING.